CH00853344

WILD WOOLLY

Three Word Challenge Series: Book 1

WRITTEN & ILLUSTRATED BY PHILLIP REED

There once was a huge cat whose name was Woolly. He had fine curly fur, but was a bit of a bully.

He took what he wanted,
but never said please.
He teased other cats,
and said they had fleas.

He only ever ate
his favourite food.
Spitting the rest out,
he was really quite rude.

He'd say, "I'm like a wild cat,
I belong in the zoo,
I do whatever I want to do!"
Everyone agreed,
as he was such a large cat,
because if you didn't,
it was on you that he sat.

One day, he was in hospital with a blister on his paw. In the next bed was a cat sipping water from a straw.

Covered in bandages
from head to toe,
So what he looked like,
Woolly did not know.
He laid there quietly
drinking from his jug,
then our pampered cat grinned
and looked quite smug.

He was feeling thirsty,
so a plan he hatched.
Then without warning,
the water jug he snatched.
He said, "I'm like a wild cat,
I belong in the zoo,
I do whatever I want to do!"

The other cat stood up,
and was incredibly tall,
then all of a sudden
Woolly felt quite small.
He had not noticed
the very large paws,
and beneath the wrappings
the incredible jaws.

The cat ripped off the bandages
from around his head,
but this was no ordinary cat
...it was a lion instead!

"I AM a wild cat," it said,
"and I AM from the zoo,
and I'm feeling hungry,
so I think I'll eat, YOU!"
The lion opened his mouth
and let out a mighty roar.
Woolly dropped the jug,
and his jaw hit the floor.

The noise was so great
it gave Woolly a fright,
that he leapt out of bed
to an incredible height.

When Woolly landed he was
in such a strange state,
that the shock to his system
had turned his fur straight.

From that day on
he was on his best behaviour,
and he ate his food,
whatever the flavour.

He promised the other cats
he would not tease,
and if he wanted something
he would say please.
That one single meeting
had forever changed his ways,
and he was nice to the other
cats for the rest of his days.

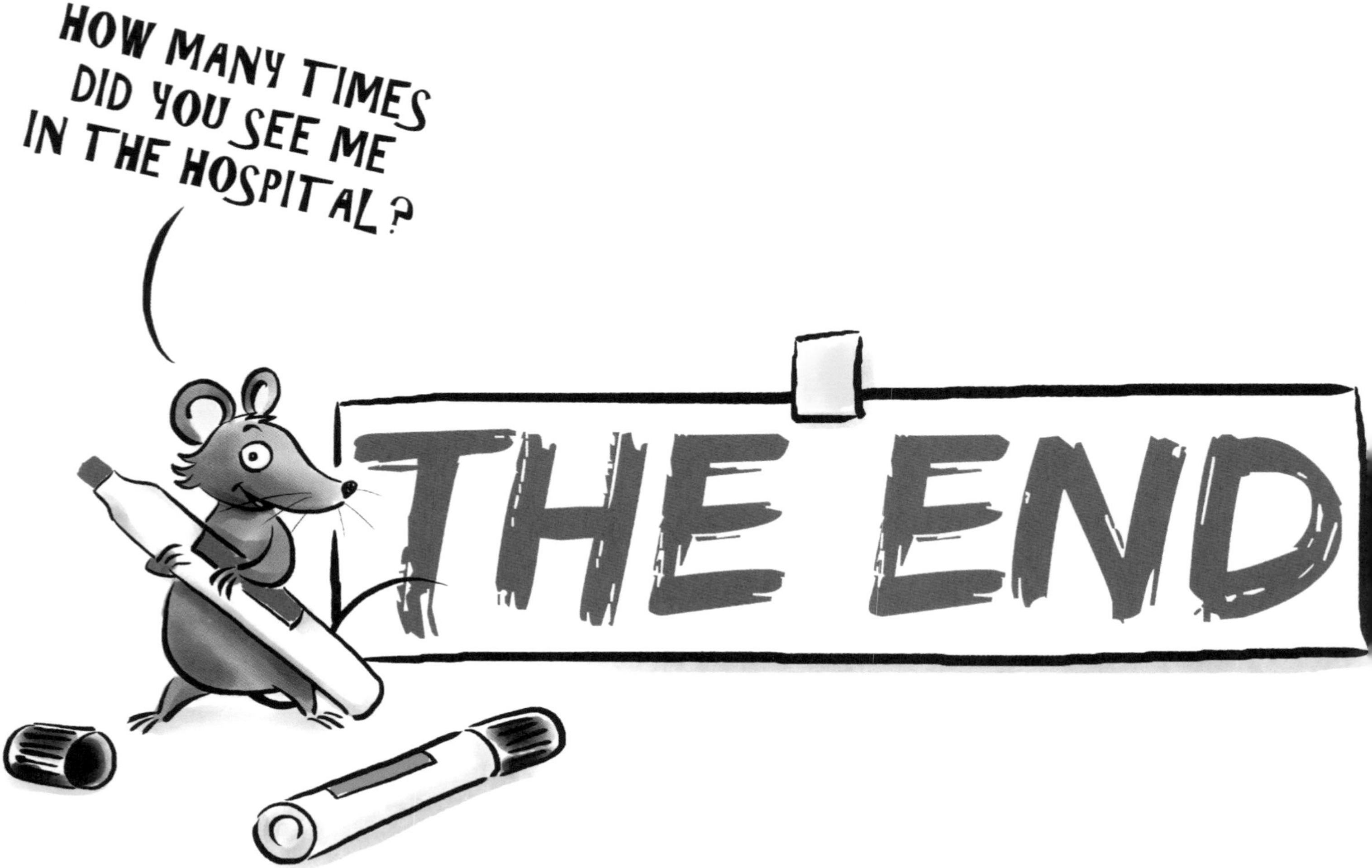
HOW MANY TIMES DID YOU SEE ME IN THE HOSPITAL?
THE END

HELP ME WRITE THE NEXT BOOK!

This story was born of three words. I like a challenge and so I asked a friend to give me

three random words and I would use them to make a picture book.

They gave me "Bully", "Lion" and "Hospital water jug"

(because they REALLY wanted to challenge me).

The result is what you have just read, which I hope you enjoyed.

Now YOU can help me write the next one.

All you need to do is email me three words* to info@phillipreed.net

If chosen, your words will be turned into a story and

you will receive a special acknowledgement in the book.

So, get thinking and get in touch.

Yours waiting with anticipation,

Phillip Reed

P.S. NO rude words or brand names please

* I'd like outrageous, varied expressions.
  Keeping each lightweight, let youngsters contribute.

Printed in Great Britain
by Amazon

69960857R00020